# Rahley the Silent Slug

# By N.D. Byma

Once upon a time, in a little bug town near a shrub and a rock, lived a slug named Rahley.

Rahley was a happy slug who enjoyed leafy food, hot tea, and the morning newspaper.

Early every morning, after putting on his safety vest and packing his lunch, Rahley would leave for work with a smile on his face.

As Rahley slithered by, other bugs would happily say "Good morning Rahley," and Rahley would wave back without saying a word. You see, what many don't know is, slugs are afraid of their own voices.

Rahley really wanted to speak but he had never heard his own voice before and didn't know what it would sound like. "What if I sound like a screeching dung beetle and everyone laughs at me?" he thought.

"Even worse, what if I'm loud like a barking spider and scare everyone?
No, it's better and safer to be a silent slug," he thought, and Rahley never made a sound.

So today, like every day, Rahley slithered down the road on his way to work and, as all the bugs said, "Hello," he only smiled and waved back.

Rahley loved his job as safety monitor at Stick Bridge beside Monument Rock. As the bus zoomed by in the morning, the bugs would yell "HELLO RAHLEY!" and Rahley would happily wave back.

Sometimes bug families and groups of school bugs would come by on family visits and school trips to look at Stick Bridge, Monument Rock and the canyon below. Rahley loved these days and pointed happily to everything he wanted the kids to see.

As the school bugs and bug families left, they would all yell "THANK YOU RAHLEY!" and, like every day before, Rahley would smile and wave goodbye back.

After every long, fun day working at Stick Bridge beside Monument Rock,
Rahley came home and relaxed with some leaves, hot tea and a good book.

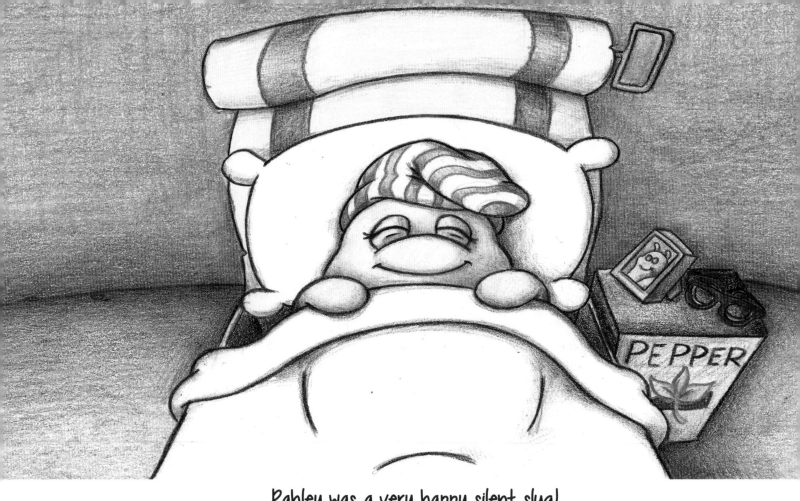

Rahley was a very happy silent slug!

One special morning, after a good sleep, Rahley started his day the usual way;
he ate breakfast, got dressed, and enjoyed his early morning slither to work.

Today was different though and Rahley knew the moment he arrived at work that something was terribly wrong! Monument Rock was gone! It had fallen over during the night and broken Stick Bridge

"OH NO!!" Rahley thought. "I need to warn the bus! It will be coming very soon and going very fast!!"Just then, he saw the bus in the distance. Rahley needed to do something quickly!

As the bus came closer, Rahley waved and jumped up and down the best any slug could, but it was no use! The driver did not see him and did not notice that the bridge was broken.

Rahley didn't have much time!

The bus was nearly at the bridge now and Rahley knew he needed to be brave.
"Here goes nothing," Rahley thought to himself and then he took a big, deep breath and yelled.

And it was the silliest voice you have ever heard.

Slamming on its brakes, the bus came to a stop right in front of Rahley. The bugs were surprised because they had never heard a slug yell before! And though it sounded silly, not a single bug laughed and not a single bug was scared.

They all asked, "What's wrong Rahley?!"

Then they saw the broken bridge.

When the bugs realized why Rahley had yelled,

they celebrated because they knew

Rahley had saved the day!

"Hurray for Rahley, the not-so-silent slug!"

they cheered.

From that day forward, all the bugs in the area knew Rahley was a hero and they would come from far away plants to hear him talk about Monument Rock and the new Stick Bridge.

Sure his voice sounded silly but Rahley didn't mind.

He loved his voice, and so did everyone else.

To everyone that reads this book,

Be proud of the voice God gave you, no matter how silly it may sound. ~ N.D. Byma

N.D. Byma lives in Beaverton, Oregon with his wonderful wife and son.

To learn more about N.D. and his previous books or to ask a question,

visit ndbyma.com or email hello@ndbyma.com